Blue Kangaroo belonged to Lily.
He was her very own kangaroo.
Sometimes Blue Kangaroo disappeared and Lily would say,
"Where are you, Blue Kangaroo?"
And Blue Kangaroo waited for Lily to find him.

One day, Lily's friend, Florence, took Lily to the park.
"Hold tight to Blue Kangaroo," said Florence.

✷ Where Are You, ✷
✷ Blue ✷
Kangaroo?

Emma Chichester Clark

HarperCollins *Children's Books*

for the one and only
Lily Brown

Collect all the fantastic books about Blue Kangaroo!

It Was You, Blue Kangaroo!

What Shall We Do, Blue Kangaroo?

I'll Show You, Blue Kangaroo!

Merry Christmas, Blue Kangaroo!

Happy Birthday, Blue Kangaroo!

Come to School Too, Blue Kangaroo!

When I First Met You, Blue Kangaroo!

First published in hardback in Great Britain by Andersen Press Ltd in 1999
First published in paperback by Picture Lions in 2001
New edition published by HarperCollins Children's Books in 2009
This edition published in 2016

15 17 19 20 18 16

ISBN: 978-0-00-710996-8

Picture Lions is an imprint of HarperCollins Publishers Ltd.
HarperCollins Children's Books is a division of HarperCollins Publishers Ltd.

Text and illustrations copyright © Emma Chichester Clark 1999

Visit our website at: www.harpercollins.co.uk

Printed in China

Lily swung on the swings, and she wasn't scared on the slide.

"I love ice-cream!" said Lily . . .

. . . and Blue Kangaroo
wondered if Lily
had forgotten him.

As they were leaving, Lily suddenly shrieked,
"Where are you, Blue Kangaroo?"
"Did you leave him on the slide?" asked Florence.

"Here he is!" smiled Lily.
"You must try to be more careful," said Florence.

The next Saturday, Lily's Aunt Jemima took Lily shopping.
"Hold tight to Blue Kangaroo," said Aunt Jemima.

On the bus, Lily met a nice lady wearing a large pink hat.

"I love buses," said Lily, as they reached their stop . . .

. . . and Blue Kangaroo wondered if he'd ever see her again.

They hadn't gone very far, when Lily shrieked,
"Where are you, Blue Kangaroo?"

"You didn't leave him on the bus, did you, Lily?"
asked Aunt Jemima.

"I think you forgot someone!" said the nice lady in the
pink hat.
"Lily!" said Aunt Jemima. "You must be more careful."

On Sunday, Uncle George took Lily to the zoo.
"Hold tight to Blue Kangaroo," said Uncle George.

"I like lions . . ." said Lily,

"... but I *love* monkeys. Can we buy them some nuts?"

And Blue Kangaroo felt very anxious.

"Shall I get six bags?" asked Lily.
"No, just one . . ." said Uncle George,

". . . and then we'll visit the real kangaroos."
But Blue Kangaroo had gone already . . .

"WHERE ARE YOU,
BLUE KANGAROO?"
shrieked Lily.

"Is that your kangaroo?" asked the zoo-keeper.
"We'd better get him back before they get
too fond of him."

"You're lucky he didn't land up with the lions," said the zoo-keeper. "Now you tuck him away somewhere safe."

That night Lily tucked Blue Kangaroo
up in bed. "We're going to the seaside
tomorrow . . ." she said, and she fell
asleep with Blue Kangaroo in her arms.

But Blue Kangaroo couldn't sleep.
He worried and worried.

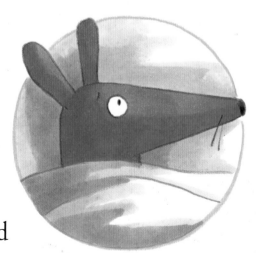

Then he slipped out of bed, and hopped
across the carpet towards the door . . .

In the morning, Lily looked everywhere for Blue Kangaroo
but she couldn't find him.

They looked in all the usual places.
"Did you leave him in the garden?" asked her mother.

Everyone searched high and low,
but Blue Kangaroo was nowhere to be found.

"It looks as if you really have lost him this time,"
said Lily's mother.

Lily ran to her room and slammed the door.
"Where, oh *where* are you, Blue Kangaroo?" she sobbed.

Lily wiped her tears away . . . and guess who she saw?
"You naughty Blue Kangaroo!" she said . . .

. . . and she never let Blue Kangaroo
out of her sight,
ever, again.